Purple Class and the
Half-Eaten Sweater

**Other titles by Sean Taylor for
Frances Lincoln Children's Books:**

Purple Class and the Skelington
Purple Class and the Flying Spider
Crocodiles are the Best Animals of All
The Great Snake: Stories from the Amazon

For Lucy, Alice and Luke
and with thanks to Lottie, George and Stan.

Purple Class and the Half-Eaten Sweater copyright © Frances Lincoln Limited 2009
Text copyright © Sean Taylor 2009
Illustrations copyright © Helen Bate 2009
The right of Sean Taylor to be identified as the author and of Helen Bate and Polly Dunbar
to be identified as the illustrators of this work has been asserted by them in accordance
with the Copyright, Designs and Patents Act, 1988 (United Kingdom)

First published in Great Britain in 2009 and in the USA in 2010 by
Frances Lincoln Children's Books, 4 Torriano Mews,
Torriano Avenue, London NW5 2RZ
www.franceslincoln.com

British Library Cataloguing in Publication Data available on request

ISBN 978-1-84507-909-3

Set in Plantin and Blockhead

Printed in the UK by CPI Bookmarque, Croydon, CR0 4TD

1 3 5 7 9 8 6 4 2

Sean Taylor

Purple Class and the Half-Eaten Sweater

and other stories

Illustrated
by Helen Bate

F
FRANCES LINCOLN
CHILDREN'S BOOKS

Contents

Purple Class and the Half-Eaten Sweater

"Sit yourselves down!" called out Mr Wellington, as the first of the children came bouncing into Purple Class. There was a chatter of voices and a scraping of feet.

It was Yasmin and Leon's turn to feed Bad Boy, the class guinea-pig. So they went across to his hutch. Bad Boy sniffed up at them. Leon unhooked the water bottle and took it to the sink. Yasmin got a handful of pellet food and dropped it in Bad Boy's bowl.

Mr Wellington picked up the register.

But instead of opening it, he wrinkled up his nose and asked, "What's that smell?"

Some of the children wrinkled their noses as well. Some of them just stared back.

"Is it perfume or something?" Mr Wellington went on.

"I've got a cold, so I can't smell," shrugged Leon, sitting down with the others.

"I can smell it and it's Shea," said Jodie.

Mr Wellington looked at Shea. So did everybody else.

"It's not *perfume*," said Shea, folding his arms. "It's Ocean Touch deodorant."

Mr Wellington puffed out his cheeks.

"You don't need deodorant at your age, do you?" he asked. Then he dropped the register on his chair and started opening the windows. "It's making this classroom smell like a flower shop on a hot afternoon!"

"My brother's got Ocean Touch deodorant!" announced Leon. "He stinks out his bedroom with it the whole time."

"You should smell the deodorant my dad uses," said Jodie. "He sprays on so much that I can smell it when I talk to him on the phone."

"But you need deodorant when you're old," pointed out Ivette. "My Mum's a beautician and she says it stops bad smells like *armpits*."

"And we don't like bad smells do we?" interrupted Mr Wellington. He picked up the register again. Ivette and her friends shook their heads. Zina said, "There are so many bad smells in the world that some days you almost wish you didn't have a nose."

A giggle spread round the class. Mr Wellington nodded. "Let's get on with our morning!" he said.

But Jamal put up his hand and announced, "I've got my own personal deodorant invention. I spray some toilet air-freshener and I run through it!"

This time the whole class burst out laughing and Mr Wellington had to hold up his hand.

"That's enough!" he called out. "And let me remind you, Jamal, you've promised to be on your very best behaviour. Otherwise you won't be taking part in our cricket session today."

Jamal nodded. "I'm going to be on the very best behaviour you've ever seen anyone do."

"Good," said Mr Wellington. He took the

register. Then he told the class, "We've got numeracy to start with. Then, who remembers who's coming in to do cricket with us?"

Ivette put her hand up. "Mike Bevington," she said.

"That's right," nodded Mr Wellington. "And what's special about Mike Bevington?"

"He once played cricket for England," replied Shea.

"He played for England *sixteen times*, in fact," pointed out Mr Wellington.

Ivette frowned. "I'd DIE of embarrassment if I had to play cricket for England," she said.

"Cricket's too slow," added Jodie.

"Well, some people say that," Mr Wellington told her. "But I think you're going to discover cricket's actually fun."

"I agree," said Jamal. "Because I'm a keen cricket enthusiast like you are, Mr Wellington."

"Thank you, Jamal," said the teacher. "And look, because we're going to be playing cricket later, I've brought in something rather special."

He reached into his bag and took out a pale sweater.

13

"This might look like any old sweater to you," he said. "But it's actually a treasured possession of mine. It was my grandfather's. And he wore it when he played for Hampshire Cricket Club."

The class leaned forward to get a better view.

"Can I feel what it's like?" asked Zina.

"Yes," nodded Mr Wellington. "Pass it quickly round."

He handed the cricket sweater to Zina, who looked at it for a moment then held it up to her nose and said, "It *stinks*."

Jodie took the sweater and sniffed it as well.

"That's disgusting," she said. "Your grandfather needed to use some Ocean Touch deodorant."

Mr Wellington gave an angry tut. "There's no need to sniff the sweater!" he said. "And there's no need to make *silly comments*!"

The children carried on passing the sweater round. Nobody said anything. But not many of them could resist giving it a little sniff either. And when it reached Leon, he squeezed his nose and shouted,

"*PWOOOOR!*"

Mr Wellington took the sweater straight back.

"That's enough!" he said. "If you can't pass the sweater around sensibly, then you're not going to touch it at all."

"Oh *man*!" groaned Jamal, "I didn't even get to smell it!"

"You're the lucky one," Jodie told him.

"QUIET!" snapped Mr Wellington. He told Yasmin to get the numeracy books out from the stationery cupboard. Then he hung the sweater from the top of one of the windows, where it was too high for the children to reach.

***

Mr Wellington had shown the class how to do bar charts the day before. Now they each had to draw one of their own. Some children chose to do a bar chart of what pets everyone in Purple Class had. And some chose to do a bar chart of how different children came to school. Mr Wellington put the numbers up on the whiteboard. Then he said, "I'm here to give a hand if anyone gets stuck."

```
What pets do we have ?
        Dog      9
        No Pet   9
        Cat      7
        Fish     3
        Snake    1
How do we get to school ?
        Walk     10
        Bus       7
        Car       7
        Bicycle   4
        Skateboard 1
```

"I've got a cousin in Australia who goes to school on a kangaroo," announced Jamal.

"That isn't funny, or clever," Mr Wellington told him. Then he started going round the tables, helping the children to get started.

Jamal fetched a pencil and a ruler. He found a fresh page in his numeracy book and drew one line up and one line across. Then he looked up at the cricket sweater.

"Leon," he whispered. "What was so wrong with the smell of that sweater?"

Leon leaned back from his work and whispered, "I don't know. But it was about the worst smell I've ever smelt. And that's with a cold."

Jamal shook his head. "Everyone got to smell it except for me," he said.

"Too late now," shrugged Leon.

"Wanna bet?" Jamal asked.

Mr Wellington was busy explaining to Zina how to start her bar chart, and Jamal stood up. Then he reached towards the sweater with his ruler. Leon squeezed his lips with his fingers to stop himself laughing. Jamal stretched and managed to get the end of the ruler into the neck of the sweater. But, as he gave it a tug, the sweater slithered down outside the window. Jamal ducked as if something had hit him on the head. Leon's glasses flashed. Both of them swung round to see if Mr Wellington had seen. But the teacher was still talking to Zina.

"You're in trouble when Mr Wellington finds out," said Leon.

"Don't tell him," Jamal whispered back. Then he jumped a little to see where the sweater had landed. It was in a litter-bin at the edge of the playground.

And just then Mr Wellington looked round.

"Jamal!" he called out. "Why are you jumping about as if you've got a bee in your underwear?"

"Sorry," said Jamal. "Can I go to the toilet?"

Mr Wellington sighed. "Go on," he said. "But make it snappy."

Jamal hurried out of the classroom. The next door along the corridor was open. Orange Class was out. There was nobody in sight. So Jamal walked on past the toilets and out down the steps. Orange Class was in the playground doing PE. Miss Zanetos was lining them up for a race between lines of cones. And underneath the Purple Class windows was the litter-bin, with the cricket sweater's sleeve dangling out of it.

Jamal walked slowly across to the bin as if a teacher had sent him. Then he took the sweater out. There was some excited shouting as the Orange Class children started their race. Miss Zanetos didn't pay any attention to Jamal.

So he turned around and walked calmly back. He wasn't really calm, though. As he went up the steps he bit his lip. Once he was in the corridor, his footsteps got faster. And that was when he noticed the sweater was wet. Something in the bin had spilled on it. Something purple. It looked like blackcurrant juice.

Jamal stopped. He had to get the sweater back into the classroom. But Mr Wellington was going to notice if he hung it back up with a big purple stain on it. So he pushed through the door into the boys' toilets. He put the sweater into a basin and turned on a tap. But the stain didn't rinse off. Jamal squeezed the soap container. There was nothing in it. The nearest place to find soap was going to be Orange Class. So, as the basin filled, he opened the door and slipped out.

The bad news was that there was a teacher outside in the corridor. Worse still, it was the head teacher, Mrs Sammy. The good news was that she was walking quickly in the other direction. So unless Jamal was unlucky, she wouldn't notice him. But Jamal *was* unlucky. As he opened the door into Orange Class, and spotted their soap by the sink, he heard Mrs Sammy's voice.

"Jamal," she called out. "What are you doing?"

Jamal spun round and stared at the head teacher as if she was a zombie.

"I'm going into Orange Class," he said.

"I can see that," Mrs Sammy told him. "And I'd like to know why."

"I thought this was our classroom," Jamal replied. "But actually it's not, is it?"

Mrs Sammy shook her head and pointed a finger at the door into Purple Class. Jamal walked in the direction her finger was pointing and Mrs Sammy followed.

All the children stopped and looked, as Jamal and the head teacher came in.

"Sorry to disturb you, Mr Wellington," said Mrs Sammy, "but I've just found Jamal wandering around the school as if he's got nothing to do."

"Well, Jamal should know better," said the teacher, with a warning tone in his voice. "His behaviour has been *dreadful* this week and he knows he'll not be playing cricket unless it improves."

Jamal sat down heavily, and Mrs Sammy left, quietly shutting the door behind her. Mr Wellington wiggled his pen between his fingers.

"Mike Bevington will be arriving in five minutes now," he told Jamal. "So you'd better make it the best-behaved five minutes of your life. Have you got me?"

Jamal put his elbows on the table. Then he said, "Not every bit of my behaviour has been dreadful has it?"

Mr Wellington sighed.

"Yesterday you were drawing a picture of a

monster-truck when you were supposed to be choosing a favourite poem to read," he said. "The day before you swung from one of the pegs and pulled it off the wall. The day before that, you spun round and round to make yourself dizzy, and knocked over half the literacy resources. And last week you pretended to be a dancing chicken at the school book fair. That's pretty dreadful as far as I'm concerned."

Jamal nodded and picked up his pencil. He wondered if he should tell Mr Wellington that his grandfather's cricket sweater was partly purple, and in the boys' toilets. He decided not to. He stared out of the window. Then he thought it would be better to stare at his numeracy book. Next to him, Bad Boy rustled in his hutch. Jamal looked across as if he wished he could disappear into some comfortable bedding himself. Then his eyes widened. Bad Boy's bedding was a sweater. And it was just about the same colour as the cricket sweater.

Three children were queuing up to show Mr Wellington their finished bar charts. He had his back turned. So Jamal reached across. He opened the catch on the lid of Bad Boy's hutch. Then he stretched his hand in and tugged out the sweater. Bad Boy scuttled backwards.

Jamal glanced across the room to make sure that Mr Wellington was still facing the other way. Then he swung the guinea-pig's sweater up so that it was hanging from the top of the open window. There were one or two wood-shavings on its sleeve. Apart from that, it looked pretty much like the cricket sweater Mr Wellington had hung there himself.

When Mr Wellington turned around, Jamal was gazing at his numeracy book with a ruler in one hand. And, at that moment, there was a loud knock at the door.

"Yes?" called out Mr Wellington. And in walked Mike Bevington.

***

The cricketer was a stocky man with a large face and cheerful eyes. He gave Mr Wellington a slap on the back, then went to the front of the class and sat on a chair that was far too small for him.

The children listened as he started by explaining what they were going to do in their cricket sessions.

"Now, am I right that you lot haven't played much cricket?" he asked. Most of the children nodded, but Jamal shook his head.

"Your worries are over," he smiled. "I play cricket all the time and I've been tipped to go to the top."

Some of the children laughed.

"Who tipped you to go to the top?" asked Ivette.

"I tipped myself," said Jamal. "I'm ready to play for England any time they want me. I'm just waiting for the phone to ring."

Mike Bevington grinned. "So you're pretty good at cricket already are you?"

Jamal gave a shrug. "That's difficult to say," he replied. "Because if I say *yes* it'll be boasting but if I say *no* it'll be lying."

"All right," interrupted Mr Wellington. "I can see Orange Class coming in from PE, so I'd like you all to get changed. Then we can get out in the playground and you can dazzle us with your amazing brilliance, Jamal."

Mike Bevington nodded and asked if there were any questions. There was only one. Leon put up his hand and asked who would win a fight between an England cricketer and a kung-fu master. Mr Wellington said it wasn't an appropriate question. Then he got the children to change and line up by the door.

Jamal looked relieved as he crossed the classroom in his PE kit. Mr Wellington hadn't noticed the sweater at all. But then the worst possible thing happened. The teacher looked round and said, "Oh! I was going to show you this, Mike!"

He strode over to the window and pulled the sweater down.

"My grandfather was a bit of a cricketer," he smiled. "This was his."

"Jolly good," nodded Mike Bevington, taking the sweater and holding it out in front of him.

The smile faded on Mr Wellington's face. The front half of the sweater looked normal, apart from some wood-shavings on the sleeve. But all that was left of the back of it were a few raggedy ends of chewed wool. Something seemed to have eaten it. Mike Bevington looked confused.

"When exactly was your grandfather playing?" he asked.

Mr Wellington scratched his head. "About forty years ago," he said.

"He used to play for a team called Hamster Cricket Club," Zina told him. Mike Bevington looked even more confused. Mr Wellington took a short breath. He was going to say something. But he never managed to because, at that moment, Ivette put up her hand and called out, "Mr Wellington! There's water coming in underneath the door."

The teacher raced across and swung open the door.

"It's coming from the boys' toilets!" he said,

and went splashing out into the corridor.

★★★

Moments later Mr Wellington was back and in his hands was the dripping cricket sweater. Jamal didn't have any choice. He had to explain everything.

"NO CRICKET FOR YOU, JAMAL!" said Mr Wellington in the sort of voice that dog trainers use. "Go to Mr Furlong's room *now*! Fetch a mop, then, while the rest of us do cricket, you can get the boys' toilets spotless and dry."

Jamal did as he was told and, a little while later, he came strolling across the playground with a mop and a bucket. Mr Wellington had hung his cricket sweater out on a wall to dry. And Mike Bevington was teaching the class some warm-up stretches. Jamal disappeared up the steps into the school and Mike Bevington explained to the children how to hold a cricket bat. Then he showed them how to make a cup with their hands to catch the ball. Then the class was split into groups to practice batting and catching.

After that, they played a training game together. Someone bowled the ball. Someone else tried to hit it in the air. And whoever managed to catch it was the next to bat. The children enjoyed it. Leon turned out to be good at batting, but Shea managed to catch him out in the end. Ivette caught the ball when Shea hit it. And it was Mr Wellington who caught out Ivette.

It was nearly time for break, but all the children wanted Mr Wellington to have his turn at batting. After a look at his watch, he said he would. The children smiled as their teacher took the bat.

"Watch out! I'm going to catch you!" said Shea.

"Me too!" called Zina, making a cup with her hands.

"It's you lot who'd better watch out," said the teacher. "I can hit that ball so hard it may catch fire in mid-air!"

"Let's see!" grinned Mike Bevington. And Yasmin bowled the ball.

Mr Wellington took a step forwards and whacked it right up into the air. It flew off and up. All the children could do was tilt back their heads and watch as it sailed above them.

"SKILL!" called out Leon.

Mr Wellington gave a slight nod as the ball arced right across the playground towards the steps into the school building. And, just then, the door opened, and down the steps came Jamal, carrying the mop and the bucket.

"MIND OUT, JAMAL!" shouted Mr Wellington.

"THE BALL!" called Ivette.

But Jamal didn't mind out. He looked up. He jumped down the last two steps. He reached out the bucket. And he caught the ball.

There was a cheer from the children, followed by clapping. Jamal walked over, fished the ball out of the bucket and threw it back to Mike Bevington.

"That was a pretty miraculous catch," said the England cricketer.

"That wasn't miraculous," said Jamal. "It was *amazing brilliance*!"

★★★

Mr Wellington told Jamal to take the bucket and mop back to Mr Furlong. He did, and when he got back the class had cleared up the cricket equipment and Mike Bevington had left. Mr Wellington fetched his cricket sweater off the wall and told the children, "I'm going back in, but you stay here for break!"

"I'm sorry about what I did," Jamal told him.

Mr Wellington looked round. "I'll bet you're sorry, Jamal," he said. "And don't forget there'll be more cricket next week. So sort yourself out. Get back in my good books. Then you'll be able to take part."

"I'm going to make sure I do," Jamal told him. "If it will help get me in your good books, I can improve the smell of that sweater by spraying some toilet air-freshener and running through holding it!"

Yasmin, Leon and several others burst out laughing. Mr Wellington shook his head.

"I sometimes wonder what ever made me work with children," he said. And the bell went for break.

The Non-Stop Fund-Raising Day

The bell had just gone at the end of morning break and Mr Wellington was standing at the front of the class dressed in his pyjamas. Saima sat near the computer table. She was the new teaching assistant who helped Mr Wellington three mornings a week. She was also wearing pyjamas.

The children in Purple Class were holding their Non-Stop Fund-Raising Day. The pyjamas were one of the ways that they were raising money. By paying one pound, anyone could come to school wearing nightclothes. So the children

arriving back from break were dressed in pyjamas too. (Except for Leon. He hadn't understood the instructions properly, and he was dressed as a bear).

The Non-Stop Fund-Raising Day was happening because of an earthquake in Turkey. A lot of people had died. Families had lost their homes. And the children had decided they wanted to help. Jodie had looked on the Internet and found out that a donation of £160 would provide a tent for eight people with water containers and a pack of toys for the children. So the aim of their Non-Stop Fund-Raising Day was to raise a grand total of £160.

As Jodie came in she said, "Break goes too quickly. Twenty minutes only lasts *one* minute."

Then Shea called out, "Mr Wellington, how much money have we got so far?"

The teacher waited for all the children to settle down. Then he picked up a piece of paper and said, "*Coming to School in Nightclothes* raised £31. Those of you who've just done the *Morning-Break Skipathon* raised another £38.20. That makes £69.20 in all."

"It's not even halfway to our grand total,"

pointed out Yasmin.

"You still need more than £90," nodded Mr Wellington.

Ivette shrugged. "But if we don't raise enough, you can always top it up with some money you've got to spare, can't you?"

Mr Wellington put his hands on his hips. "Money I've got to spare? Who says I've got money to spare?"

There was a moment's quiet. Then Zina told him, "Everyone."

Ivette nodded. "Everyone says your father owns the factory that makes Wellington boots. So you've got a platinum credit card and a luxury house with a waterfall going down into the bathtub."

"Well, I'm sorry to disappoint everyone," Mr Wellington told her, "but my father doesn't have anything to do with Wellington boots. I don't have a platinum credit card. And I live in a very ordinary house."

"Haven't you even got a bathtub with a waterfall going down into it?" asked Zina.

"No," Mr Wellington told her. "So it's going to be up to all of *you* to raise the money."

Some of the children looked a little let down, so Saima told them, "Don't worry. You've still got your *Smoothie Sale* and your *Friendship Bracelet Stall* to come at lunchtime."

Mr Wellington nodded. "And Shea and Jamal are going to be doing their *Clean a Teacher's Car Service*. So, unless there are unforeseen problems, I think you're going to raise your £160."

Shea put up his hand. "There is a slightly unforeseen problem," he said. "I was going to borrow my dad's car-cleaning things, but I didn't manage to because I forgot."

Mr Wellington sighed and put his hands in his pyjama pockets. "Yesterday you wouldn't stop going on about all the different bodywork shampoos you were going to bring in, Shea," he said.

"I could have got them," Shea replied. "But, you see, last night I borrowed some extra-realistic plastic dog poo from my cousin, and it distracted me."

"*Extra-realistic plastic dog poo?*" frowned Mr Wellington.

Shea nodded. "It's shiny as if it's just freshly done..."

"All right," interrupted the teacher.

"I put it in my mum's mashed potato and she made a face as if she was going to cry," went on Shea. "Then I put it on my sister's bed…"

"SHEA!" said Mr Wellington, firmly. "THAT'S ENOUGH! I'm not the slightest bit interested in the plastic dog poo, or what you did with it. What I'm interested in is how you and Jamal are going to contribute to our Non-Stop Fund-Raising Day."

Shea fiddled with his shirt collar. "I'm not doing sponsored skipping," he said.

"Nor am I," added Jamal.

"That's all right," Mr Wellington told them. "But you're going to do *something*."

"Sponsored wearing a baseball cap?" suggested Jamal.

Mr Wellington shook his head. "No one's going to sponsor you for doing something that takes no effort. If you want to be sponsored you have to do something impressive."

"Sponsored hotdog eating," suggested Shea.

Jamal nodded. "I could eat about thirty hotdogs in five minutes. That's impressive."

Mr Wellington shook his head again.

"You'd have to *buy* the hotdogs. And how much would that cost?"

A hairy paw went up. It was Leon.

"At my brother's youth club they did sponsored wearing your pants on your head," he said.

Everyone laughed, except for Mr Wellington. "And?" he asked. "Did they raise much money?"

Leon shook his head. "I think people spent more time laughing at them than giving them money."

Around the classroom lots of children started talking about wearing their pants on their heads, and Mr Wellington had to call out, "Quiet!"

The chatting didn't stop. So he shouted, "SILENCE!"

And Zina's face lit up. She put up her hand and called out, "They could do a sponsored *silence*!"

"*That* would be impressive," nodded Mr Wellington. He looked at the boys and added. "I'd make a donation of £10 if you two could keep quiet for half an hour."

"HALF AN HOUR!" blurted out Jamal.

"I could do about six minutes."

"Half an hour is DIFFICULT!" complained Shea.

"Of course it's difficult," said the teacher. "That's the point."

Shea turned his mouth down. "I could do it though," he went on. "I can do almost anything if I try. Yesterday I chewed my sandwich into the shape of a quad-bike and it looked just like the real thing."

Jamal nodded in agreement, and Mr Wellington told the boys, "That's decided then. You two can do a sponsored silence at lunchtime. Now we've got important things to get on with."

He reached down and picked up a box full of bananas and limes.

"Zina's father has kindly donated this fruit from his shop," he said. "And half of you are going to work with me making banana and lime smoothie for our *Smoothie Sale*. The other half will be making friendship bracelets with Saima."

***

The friendship bracelet makers stayed in the classroom, and Mr Wellington took the rest of the class through the hall to the kitchens. Linda, the dinner lady, was there.

"What are you going to need, to make this smoothie stuff?" she asked.

"We did it in Cooking Club," said Ivette. "For each banana you add half a cup of milk and a spoon of lime juice. Then you just *moosh* it up in a blender."

Linda reached into a cupboard and found a blender. Then she took out a great big pan for them to serve the finished smoothie from. Mr Wellington got the children to wash their hands. Then he organised them into groups. Jodie's group had to peel the bananas. Leon's group was going to chop them. Yasmin's group had to do the lime squeezing. Shea's group had to measure out the milk. And Ivette's group was in charge of the blending.

"Don't we need safety goggles?" asked Jodie.

"Not for peeling bananas, Jodie," Mr Wellington told her.

Some of the groups worked at a kitchen counter and some of them sat at a table. Leon said he could chop a banana like a TV chef, and got everyone to watch.

"Have you done some cooking before?" Mr Wellington asked.

"I tried to fry an egg on the living room radiator once," Leon replied. The children sitting at his table burst out laughing.

"Did that work?" chuckled Mr Wellington.

Leon shook his head and said, "My mum had to get in professional carpet cleaners."

He tipped chopped banana into the blender and, not long after, Ivette was pouring out the first lot of finished smoothie. Mr Wellington looked pleased.

"Many hands make light work," he said, and he let the children try what they'd made.

Ivette said she liked it. Yasmin didn't look so sure. And Jodie said, "Whoever invented that flavour needs to get their head fixed! It tastes like banana and *SLIME*!"

"Don't be silly," Mr Wellington told her. And he tasted some of the smoothie himself. "That's not bad."

"It's nice," nodded Linda.

"Now!" went on Mr Wellington. "Time is ticking. You've all brought in packed lunches so that we can eat early and run our stalls at lunchtime. Let's get on with this quickly and sensibly!"

The children were quite sensible. But they weren't quick. Shea sat on a banana. Leon laughed so much that he fell off his chair. Yasmin squirted lime juice in her eye and said she was going to have to go to hospital. And Jodie pointed out, "I knew we should have used safety goggles."

Then the other group arrived to set up their *Friendship Bracelet Stall* on the stage. And everyone wanted to stop and see the bracelets (including Yasmin, whose eye was now better).

By the time the smoothie was finally ready, the bracelet makers had gone back to the classroom to have their lunches. Ivette and Leon carried the pan carefully to a table by the stage, and Linda brought across a serving ladle. Mr Wellington asked the children to thank her. He said he'd stay to organise the cups. Then he sent the group to join the others back in the classroom.

★★★

When they got back, Saima was leaving because she had to look after Blue and Yellow Classes.

"Find your lunches if you've just arrived!" she called out. "Mr Wellington will be back in just a moment. And I want everyone sitting quietly when he gets here."

Once she'd gone, Jamal rocked back on his chair and called out, "Shea! Look!"

He held up a sign that he'd made. It said,

JAmAl andSheA's
deAdLy difficult
sponsored SILENCE

"That's good," nodded Shea, and he sat down with his packed lunch. Then he went on, "Look what I got my mum to give me. Chocolate biscuits. A chocolate-spread sandwich. And a bar of chocolate!"

He snapped open his lunchbox. Then he made a face as if he was going to cry. On his sandwich was a twist of fresh-looking dog poo.

There was a cackle of laughter from Jamal

and the others sitting at the table.

"Your mum got you back, Shea!" grinned Zina.

Then Jodie called out, "Trick Mr Wellington with that!"

"Trick Mr Wellington!" echoed Jamal. Shea took a bite of his sandwich. Then he said, "All right."

"Quickly!" said Jamal.

"Put it in his briefcase!" called out Jodie.

"No," said Zina. "Put it in his top drawer!"

"He won't even open his drawer," tutted Ivette. "Put it on his chair!"

"Just leave it on his desk!" hissed Jamal.

Shea's eyes shifted from place to place, but it was too late. Yasmin called out, "He's coming!"

And, almost at once, Mr Wellington walked back in.

"Everything's set up now," he said. "And the bell will be going. So finish your packed lunches. Then those of you who are in charge of the stalls can go to the hall."

Jamal held up his sign and said, "I did this!"

"Good," said Mr Wellington.

"Can I go with Jamal and put the sign up?" Shea asked.

"All right," the teacher nodded. "Choose a place to do your sponsored silence and put up the sign. We'll join you in a minute or two."

***

As the boys headed up the corridor, Jamal told Shea, "You were slow! You should have put that dog poo somewhere quickly. Then it would have been funny."

Shea pushed open the door into the hall. The dinner tables had been set out and there was a clinking of plates and cutlery from the kitchens.

"I wasn't slow!" he said. "I didn't have time!"

"You were slow!" laughed Jamal.

"I wasn't!" said Shea. Then he took the plastic dog poo out of his pocket and chucked it at Jamal. It missed. It hit the corner of the *Smoothie Sale* table and bounced into the air. And Shea stared, wide-eyed, as it dropped into the pan of smoothie.

"Where did it go?" asked Jamal.

"In there!" said Shea, rushing over to the pan. Jamal tried not to laugh as he followed.

"Can you see it?" he asked. Shea shook his head.

"It's sunk," he said.

Jamal hitched up his pyjama bottoms and grinned into the pan.

"Get it before Mr Wellington comes!" he said.

Shea picked up the serving ladle but, as he did, the bell went. "They're coming!" he whispered. Then he dipped the ladle into the smoothie and fished around.

"Can you find it?" Jamal asked.

Shea pulled a face and lifted out the ladle. The only thing in it was banana and lime smoothie. He tried again. This time the ladle touched against something hard. He lifted it.

"There it is!" said Jamal.

The twist of dog poo was balancing half on and half off the ladle. Shea lifted it carefully. But the dog poo toppled and dropped. He tried to scoop it back up, but the door into the hall opened.

It was Mr Wellington with the children.

"Excuse me!" the teacher's voice said. "What are you two doing?"

Shea rotated the ladle a couple of times. "This smoothie mixture needed a bit of a stir," he replied.

"Have you chosen a place to do your sponsored silence?" Mr Wellington asked. Neither of the boys answered.

"Don't just stare at me at me like a pair of stuffed mummies," said the teacher.

"We can do it on the stage," said Jamal. Mr Wellington nodded.

"Then go and sit there until we're ready to start."

As he spoke, a stream of Blue and Yellow Class children arrived for lunch with Saima. Jodie, Ivette and Leon took charge of the *Smoothie Sale*. Zina and some others stood behind the *Friendship Bracelet Stall*.

"I'm going to be embarrassed," said Shea, as he sat down next to Jamal up on the stage.

"You'll be more embarrassed when Mr Wellington finds out where that dog poo is," Jamal told him. Shea looked down into the pan of smoothie.

"It's sunk right to the bottom," he said. "And they're never going to sell much of it."

But he was wrong. Soon quite a little line of children was queuing up at the *Smoothie Sale* table.

"Right boys!" came Mr Wellington's voice. "Are you going to manage this sponsored silence?"

"I can do it about twenty times in a row," said Jamal.

"Well, let's see," Mr Wellington told him. Then he called across the hall, "LISTEN EVERYONE! SHEA AND JAMAL ARE GOING TO START A SPONSORED SILENCE!"

Children turned round to look. Mr Wellington checked his watch.

"RIGHT! THE HALF AN HOUR STARTS NOW!" he said.

Jamal nodded and asked, "Are we allowed to talk if it's so quietly that no one can hear?"

"No," Mr Wellington told him, and Jodie said, "Jamal just spoke something, so he's out!"

"We haven't started yet," complained Jamal.

"Now you spoke again!" pointed out Jodie.

"Never mind," said Mr Wellington. "RIGHT! WE'RE STARTING AGAIN... NOW!"

Jamal said, "This time I'm going to stay completely silent."

"*You've got to stop talking, Jamal!*" complained Shea.

"Now Shea's out too!" announced Jodie.

Shea threw a hand in the air and told Mr Wellington, "Jodie keeps distracting us!"

Mr Wellington shook his head.

"Look," he said, "If people distract you, I suggest you just point at your mouth and shake your head to show that you can't speak."

The boys nodded.

"RIGHT!" said Mr Wellington, for the third time, "WE'LL START PROPERLY... NOW!"

This time the minutes passed and the boys didn't speak. Some older children from Red Class and Green Class came in for lunch. They made comments and asked questions to try to get the boys to speak. But it didn't work. Shea and Jamal pointed at their mouths and shook their heads. And their lips stayed sealed. Ten minutes passed. Twenty minutes passed. Linda and the other dinner ladies served up lunch. The last of the children from other classes arrived. It looked as if the boys were going to manage. Then the door into the hall opened and in walked Mrs Sammy with the school's Chair of Governors, Mr Miah.

***

The two visitors walked across to Mr Wellington. Mr Miah seemed a little surprised to be shaking hands with a teacher dressed in pyjamas, but he didn't say anything. He looked around and smiled.

"I've just had lunch with Mr Miah," Mrs Sammy explained, "and I thought he might like to contribute to your fund-raising activities."

Mr Wellington nodded gratefully at the Chair of Governors. Then he said, "The children have worked hard, and we hope to raise a grand total of £160."

Mr Miah raised his eyebrows. "Well done!" he said.

"That's a stall selling friendship bracelets,"

went on the teacher. "Those boys are doing a sponsored silence. And these children are selling cups of smoothie. Perhaps you'd like one?"

Shea peered down into the pan.

"Mmm," smiled Mr Miah glancing into the pan himself. "I'll certainly buy a cup. What flavour is it?"

"Banana and slime," said Mr Wellington. "I mean banana and *lime*."

"Very tasty," nodded Mr Miah, and he reached into his pocket for some coins.

Ivette scooped down to the bottom of the pan and filled a cup with smoothie mixture. Shea leaned forwards. There was no sign of the dog poo.

"Delicious," said Mr Miah, sipping the smoothie. "And tell me, Mr Wellington, how close to their grand total have the children got?"

"Good question," replied Mr Wellington. "Give me a moment and I'll tell you."

He went to check how much the two stalls had taken, and came back just as Mr Miah drank the last of his smoothie.

"QUIET EVERYONE!" he shouted. "Mr

Miah has asked how close we are to reaching our target of £160. And I'm pleased to say we've now raised £152.70!"

The Chair of Governors started clapping and everyone in the hall joined in. Mr Wellington looked at his watch. Then he called out, "Shea and Jamal's sponsored silence will raise another £10 if they can stay quiet for the next *four* minutes. And with that £10 we'll reach our grand total!"

Mr Miah smiled at the boys. "You can do it!" he nodded. "And let me do my bit by buying another cup of this delicious smoothie."

He paid Leon. Ivette dipped the ladle into the pan. And, with a messy plop, the plastic dog poo dropped into the cup.

***

This time it was Mr Wellington who made a face as if he was going to cry.

"Dear me!" called out the Chair of Governors. He reached into the cup and lifted out the

glistening twist of dog poo. Mrs Sammy's eyes widened.

"It's a piece of plastic dog's whotsit!" said Mr Miah. Then he handed it to Mrs Sammy.

"Oh my gosh!" gasped the head teacher. "That's absolutely *disgusting*!"

Mr Wellington wetted his lips. "Yes," he nodded, "It's shiny as if it's just freshly done."

Mr Miah and Mrs Sammy stared at Mr Wellington. He looked as though he wished he hadn't said what he'd just said. Then the head teacher called out, "Who's responsible for this? Come on! Own up!"

Mr Wellington turned straight to Shea and Jamal. They looked back at him. Then Shea pointed at his mouth and shook his head. And Jamal did the same. Mrs Sammy put the plastic poo down on the table and looked around herself.

"Mr Wellington, find out who this horrible thing belongs to!" she said.

"Actually..." smiled Mr Wellington. "It's all part of our Non-Stop Fund-Raising Day fun. You see, there's a free gift for the lucky person who gets the dog poo in their cup. Shea and Jamal will wash your car whenever you like for the rest of term!"

"Oh," nodded Mr Miah.

"I see," said Mrs Sammy, looking relieved.

"That's right isn't it, boys?" asked Mr Wellington. And Shea and Jamal blinked back. They couldn't say anything to disagree.

Two minutes later, there was a cheer

as Mr Wellington counted down the end of the successful sponsored silence. Mrs Sammy and Mr Miah congratulated everyone in the class. Then they walked out, leaving Mr Wellington alone with the children.

"Half an hour's sponsored silence is probably a world record for someone my age isn't it?" said Jamal. But Mr Wellington wasn't paying much attention. He was looking at Shea and holding out the plastic dog poo. Shea reached down and took it. He started explaining how it had ended up in the pan of smoothie. But Mr Wellington interrupted him.

"I'm really not interested, Shea," he told him. "Just give it back to your cousin and make sure I *never* see it again. The main thing is that you managed your sponsored silence and we've reached our grand total in one day."

The children looked pleased with themselves, and Jodie said, "With a bit of luck there'll be another earthquake soon and we can do a Non-Stop Fund-Raising Day again."

Shea nodded. "And next time," he said, "we two can do a sponsored silence with our pants on our heads!"

The Underwear Wolf

With a slow hiss, the door of the coach floated open.

"Right. On you get," said Mr Wellington.

It was the week of the Purple Class school journey. They were going to the Hillcrest Outdoor Activity Centre.

"Find yourself a seat and sit down!" called out the teacher as Zina went past wearing a pair of wrap-around sunglasses. She was followed by Yasmin, Shea, then Jodie in a fluffy coat, and Saima, who was the other member of staff going

on the coach. Mrs Sammy and Jodie's mum were also coming on the trip. But they were going to arrive by car in the morning.

Mr Wellington was the last one on. He was carrying a bag of apples and a tray of drinkable yoghurts. Most of the children were sitting down, but Leon was standing up rotating his waist and jigging from foot to foot.

"Leon!" said the teacher. "When I say *sit down* I mean *SIT DOWN*. I'm sorry if it's confusing."

"Do you know what this is I'm doing?" Leon asked.

"You look like someone trying to put on a pair of trousers on a bouncy castle," Mr Wellington told him. Leon shook his head.

"It's Hawaiian hip-dancing," he beamed.

"Very nice, Leon," Mr Wellington told him. "Now sit down."

Leon lowered himself into the seat next to Shea and, from a few rows back, Jamal called out, "These seats are too soft!"

Mr Wellington didn't hear. Or he pretended that he didn't hear. He was counting the children.

"Our school should get a corporate jet to take

us on school journeys," announced Ivette.

"I'll suggest it at the next staff meeting," Mr Wellington replied. He finished counting and told the driver. "That's everyone."

Then he sat down at the front, and the coach went gliding away from the school.

After a few moments Yasmin put up her hand and asked, "Can we have the snacks you've got us?"

Mr Wellington looked around.

"Not for now," he said.

"How long is *not for now*?" asked Leon.

"You can have your snacks once we're about halfway there," Mr Wellington told him. The coach pulled out into the main road and started to pick up speed. In the seat behind Mr Wellington, Jodie rolled up her fluffy coat and put her head on it as if it was a pillow.

"What's it going to be like when we get there?" she asked.

Mr Wellington looked round again.

"A lot of fun," he told her.

"Does that mean we can have a water fight with wet toilet paper?" called out Jamal. Mr Wellington shook his head.

"How about an all-night rave party?" suggested Zina.

Mr Wellington shook his head again.

"You should let us have an all-night rave party," Leon told him. "Then you can witness some more of my Hawaiian hip-dancing."

"I'm sure that would be worth staying up all night for," said Mr Wellington, "but we've got other treats waiting for us. The Hillcrest Centre is an amazing place in the middle of the woods, with a climbing wall, a zip wire, a kayaking lake, real chickens in a real chicken coop..."

"And a werewolf," said Zina.

"Yeah, there's a werewolf," agreed Shea.

"That's just a silly story," said Mr Wellington.

"It isn't," Zina told him. "My sister, Khadija, saw a werewolf when she went..."

"Khadija was just imagining things," interrupted Mr Wellington.

"That's not what she told me," pointed out Zina, and she stared at the teacher through her wrap-around sunglasses. "She said it was an actual werewolf from the woods with hairy shoulders."

"My dad's got hairy shoulders," said Ivette.

"So's mine," Yasmin told her. "It's disgusting."

"But your dads aren't werewolves, are they?" said Mr Wellington. "And there's no werewolf where we're going."

Lots of children were listening now, and Ivette pointed out, "Teachers just say that all the time, even when there is a werewolf."

"My brother said there was one when he went!" nodded Shea. "Someone saw a werewolf in the boys' room. Then, in the morning, my brother's pants had completely mysteriously disappeared from his bag."

There was a burst of laughter from the children.

Mr Wellington looked at Shea and asked, "So are you telling me there's a werewolf at the Hillcrest Centre that goes around wearing your brother's pants?"

There was an even bigger burst of laughter. Shea shrugged.

"It's anyone's guess," he said. "All I know is they were brand new Spiderman boxer-shorts, and no one has ever seen them again since the werewolf took them."

Jodie lifted her head off her fluffy coat and said, "It's an *underwearwolf*!"

Some of the children screamed. Some of them laughed. Some of them laughed and screamed.

"Quiet!" called out Mr Wellington. "There's no such thing as a werewolf! Or an underwearwolf! And there's nothing to be scared of at the Hillcrest Centre. In fact, one of the first things we'll be doing is going for a night-hike in the woods."

"In the dark?" asked Ivette.

"Yes," Mr Wellington nodded. "Now I suggest we change the subject."

"Can we have those snacks you brought us?" asked Yasmin.

"Good idea," said the teacher.

★★★

A few minutes later Mr Wellington went past giving out apples. Saima followed, handing everyone a drinkable yogurt. And soon the children were crunching apples and sucking at straws.

Jodie turned to Zina and asked. "What's a werewolf like if we do see one?"

"It's the scariest thing ever found, ever," Zina told her. "It comes out if there's a full moon. It's got long greasy hair, a long greasy tail, and long greasy teeth."

"And it runs at fifty miles an hour," added Shea.

"I'd run at fifty miles an hour if I saw something like that," said Ivette from the seat behind.

"But if you run at sixty miles an hour it will be no good," Zina told her, "because the werewolf can still kill you in the worst way imaginable."

The children looked at her.

"How?" asked Leon.

"My sister told me," said Zina. "But I don't want to say it, because it will probably make Yasmin sick on the coach."

"I don't get sick on the coach any more," complained Yasmin. "That was just when I was a child."

"Tell us then, Zina," said Jodie.

"All right," she nodded. "*First it chases you until it kills you. Then it drags you to pieces with its claws. Then it eats you up, bones and all!"*

"UUUUUUUUURGH!" went everyone sitting around her.

"It's true," said Shea. "I saw it on *Dawn of the Dead.*"

"I've seen that," pointed out Ivette.

Shea looked round.

"I watch it every night," he told her.

The coach reached the motorway. Saima collected apple cores and empty yoghurt cartons in a bag. And Mr Wellington went past with a packet of wet-wipes. Most of the children took one to clean their fingers. But Jamal shook his head.

"I don't use wet-wipes," he said. "In my opinion they're for babies."

They went through a valley covered with tall, straight trees and came to open fields. They passed some white horses near a house, and all the children wanted to see them. Then the driver left the motorway and headed up a narrow road. Two or three miles along it they reached a sign saying HILLCREST OUTDOOR ACTIVITY CENTRE, and the coach pulled up.

When Zina stepped off, she could see green hills one way and trees the other way. Mr Wellington handed out bags from the luggage compartment, and Zina asked him, "Is this where we've got to sleep?"

The teacher shook his head as he held out her rucksack.

"This is the car park," he said. "The Hillcrest Centre is up that track."

Shea looked towards the trees. Then he said, "I can feel an eerie chill in the air... as if something evil is watching us."

Jodie hugged her rucksack to her chest, and Leon asked, "If a werewolf eats you up, bones and all, Mr Wellington, which bus do we catch to get home?"

"I've got more important things to do than be eaten by a werewolf, Leon," the teacher told him. Then he made sure everyone was ready and led the class up the track.

Trees rose high above them on both sides. Some children raced ahead. Some walked slowly behind because their bags were heavy. Mr Wellington and Saima both had to shout to make sure the class stuck together. Ivette spotted a clump of stinging nettles, and Mr Wellington warned the children to watch out for them. But Jamal was pretending he'd lost his eyesight in a jungle war and he got stung on the leg.

"Those nettle things should be banned," frowned Zina. Jamal said he wanted a wet-wipe for the sting. Then Ivette found some footprints and said they were werewolf tracks, and Mr Wellington had to go back and see the footprints.

"I'd say those were made by a small dog like a poodle," he told the children.

"How do you know they're not werewolf tracks?" asked Zina.

"Because they're tiny, Zina!" Mr Wellington told her.

"It might be a mini-werewolf," Zina blinked back.

Mr Wellington looked as if he'd quite like to go home. But, just then, a tall man with dark hair and a bristly beard came round a curve in the track. Some of the children looked a bit startled. But the stranger shook Mr Wellington by the hand. Then he said, "Welcome to the Hillcrest

Centre, Purple Class. I'm Jim Knight. My wife and I run this place."

***

Jim Knight led the children on up the track, and Ivette and Jamal asked him about what they'd be doing.

"Tomorrow I'll be getting you up our climbing wall," he told them. "Then, if the weather's bright, we'll go out on the kayaking lake."

"That sounds good to my ears," said Jamal. "Because I'm into extreme sports. And I'm also good at basketball and wrist-wrestling. And I can fix quad-bike engines."

Round the curve in the track was the Hillcrest Centre building. Jim Knight led them round it and past a chicken coop. Then they came to a pair of chalets. The one near the chickens was for the girls. Across the path was one for the boys.

"This is where we'll be sleeping," said Saima, as the girls followed her into their chalet.

"It smells of mashed potatoes," complained Jodie.

"Don't be silly," Saima told her, opening

a window. There were bunk beds against the walls. There was a separate teacher's bedroom.

And there was a bathroom with toilets and showers. The girls chose beds and put down their things. Jodie climbed on to a top bunk by a window. Ivette said she had to take her cough medicine. And Zina asked Saima, "Would you rather be dragged to pieces by a werewolf's claws, stung to death by killer bees or thrown into a snake pit?"

Saima told her, "I'm hoping none of those things happens."

Then she called out, "I'm going to fetch Ivette's cough medicine from Mr Wellington. Behave yourselves and start unpacking while I'm gone."

As she left, Zina kicked off her trainers. Then she tried skidding across the floor. But she didn't go far.

"It's dirty," said Yasmin, fetching a broom that was leaning against the wall. She started sweeping the floor, and Zina clambered on to the top bunk next to Jodie's.

"Your feet smell of cheese!" Jodie told her.

"THEY DON'T!" frowned Zina. "I put aromatherapy oil on them every night!"

Then Yasmin swept a dusty pair of socks out from under one of the beds.

"Smell these!" she grinned, and chucked the socks at Zina. There was a burst of laughter. Zina shouted, "YEEEUCK!"

Then she flicked the socks at Jodie. Jodie was

going to throw them straight back but, before she could, Zina dropped off her bunk and ran out of the chalet. Jodie leaned towards the open window and, as Zina appeared, she threw the socks. They hit her on the top of the head, and the girls who saw it fell about laughing. Zina bent down and tried to throw the socks back. But they went in the air, landed on the roof, and didn't come down.

"You've got to get them, Zina!" called Ivette. "Otherwise the underwearwolf is going to climb up there in the night."

Zina skipped back a few paces to see the socks. But Saima was coming.

"Zina!" she called out. "Did I ask you to start dancing round the chicken coop with no shoes on?"

Zina shook her head.

"Then in you go," Saima told her.

It wasn't long before dinner-time. When they went to the dining room they met Mrs Knight and the Hillcrest Centre's ginger cat, which was called Goggles.

Mrs Knight asked if anyone had any special dietary requirements. Shea put up his hand and told her, "I like mini-doughnuts."

But Mr Wellington told him that wasn't what Mrs Knight wanted to know. Then they had pizza, salad and garlic bread. It was getting dark by the time they'd finished. The children did the cleaning up and, when they were all back in their places, Mr Wellington said, "Right, it's time to go on our night–hike."

He sent the children back to the chalets to put on their coats and outdoor shoes. Then they gathered on the path. Beams of light danced in the air because Mr Wellington, Saima and several of the children had torches.

"OK! Listen," called out the teacher, "*I* know where we're going, so I want everyone to stay behind me. And keep your voices down because there are badgers, rabbits and all sorts of other animals living in the woods."

Then they set off down the path.

Jodie walked in between Zina and Ivette and, as they reached the edge of the woods, the three of them linked arms. Trees stood around them like black ghosts. There was just a breath of breeze shifting the tops of the branches now and then.

"Don't worry!" called out Jamal. "If we see the underwearwolf I'm going to scare it off with some kung-fu moves."

"If we see it, my heart is going to stop big-time!" said Jodie.

"Your hair might turn white in one moment," remarked Zina. "That's actually happened to people when they've seen a werewolf."

Leon nodded. "It happened to my nan, I think," he said.

Jodie hugged her fluffy coat around her.

"There's no way I'm going home from this school journey with white hair," she told her friends.

But they didn't see a werewolf. The woods were quiet and not actually very frightening. Stars cast a silvery light on the path and, when they were in the very thick of the trees, Mr Wellington told everyone to turn off their torches. They stood for a few moments looking up at the sky and listening to the sounds of the leaves. Nobody saw anything spooky. And when Jodie pointed out a full moon rising and Shea went "OWOOOO!" it seemed funny rather than scary. The only person who had any problem was

Zina. She walked into a tree. But it was probably because she was still wearing her wraparound sunglasses.

Back at the chalets, Mr Wellington said it had been one of the best night-hikes he could remember.

"You've been through the woods and you're back safely," he told the children. "And that's because there's nothing to be scared of."

Then he said goodnight to the girls and led the boys over to their chalet.

***

Saima locked the door as the last of the girls streamed into their room. They pulled off their coats and everyone seemed pleased to be back. Jodie lay down on her top bunk. Ivette announced that she was going to have a shower. And Saima said she'd help Yasmin, because she didn't know how to unpack her sleeping bag. Then there was a shriek. It was Jodie.

"There it is out there!" she yelped. "There!"

Every girl in the room spun round. Some of them turned to the right window. Some of them turned to the wrong window. Only Zina was quick enough to catch a glimpse of a dark figure dropping over the side of the moonlit chicken coop.

Saima rushed straight across and drew the curtains to stop the panic. But it was too late. Frightened voices filled the room. Girls stood around with hands up to their faces.

"Whatever you saw, Jodie, it wasn't a werewolf," said Saima.

"It was... definitely!" Jodie gabbled back.

"I saw it too," said Zina. "It was the underwearwolf climbing into the chicken coop! That's what my sister saw it doing!"

Saima shook her head.

"You're imagining the whole thing," she said. "There's nothing to worry about."

"Look through the curtains and you'll see it!" Jodie told her.

"All right," said Saima, and everyone stared without blinking as she walked across and opened one of the curtains.

"There's nothing there," she said. "Just the chickens."

But, at that moment, there was a scritch-scratching sound from above them. Jodie clenched her fingers into fists.

"It's on the roof!" said Zina.

"It's come for the socks!" gasped Ivette.

There was a terrible silence.

"Has my hair gone completely white?" asked Jodie. Ivette looked and shook her head. Then there was a louder scuffling sound.

"It's right above us!" yelped Jodie.

The eerie sound continued. Then, all at once, it stopped.

"It's dropped down!" whispered Zina. "It's coming to the door!"

The girls' twisted round. Everyone looked at the door handle. And, straightaway, it rattled. Ivette jumped as if a snake had bitten her. The room filled with screams. There was a bang on the door. Then the girls heard a voice.

"What's going on in there?"

It was Mr Wellington.

★★★

Saima rushed across, unlocked the door and let the teacher in.

"Was that *you* on our roof, Mr Wellington?" asked Zina. The teacher blinked.

"*Me on your roof?*" he said. "What would I be doing on your roof?"

"Well if it wasn't you, then it must have been the underwearwolf," Jodie told him.

Mr Wellington took a long breath and, as he did, there was a thud from directly above them.

"That's it," whispered Ivette. Zina looked at Mr Wellington and told him, "You've got to climb up there and wrestle the underwearwolf to the ground. You're our teacher and it's the only hope left."

Mr Wellington gave a disappointed sigh, but he said, "All right. I'll go and look."

Then he picked up a chair to stand on.

***

Saima followed him outside, and several girls huddled in the doorway, watching.

"Next time I go on a school journey I'm staying at home," announced Yasmin.

"SHHH!" Mr Wellington told her, looking up on to the roof and trying to listen.

"I can hear its hairy shoulders moving," said Zina.

"Don't be so silly," said Mr Wellington, and he climbed on to the chair. Then, using the metal drainpipe and gutter, he managed to pull himself on to the roof.

"In a few years they're going to invent personal jet-packs and then this sort of thing will be easier," commented Ivette. She and one or two other girls had stepped out into the darkness to get a better view. And some boys were appearing too. When Shea found out what was going on, he picked up a stick and held it like a spear. Mr Wellington was up on the roof, lying flat on his stomach.

"Can you see it?" whispered Zina.

"Do you want to know what I can see?" came the teacher's voice. Zina and the others nodded. Mr Wellington pushed himself into a crouching position and looked around.

"It's the cat," he said.

As he spoke, sure enough, Goggles appeared at the edge of the roof and stared at the children.

"I hope that puts your minds at ease," said Mr Wellington, and he started to climb down. He got to the drainpipe again. But, as he did, the pocket of his coat got snagged around the end of the gutter. He edged sideways to unhook it, but his foot slipped. He lost his balance and there was a gasp from the children. He only had one hand on the roof and it looked as if he was going to fall. But his coat was so firmly snagged to the gutter that he hung there.

Saima told the children not to laugh. But she was almost laughing herself. She got on the chair and tried to help Mr Wellington but she wasn't tall enough. Shea reached up with his stick, but that wasn't any help. Then, out of the darkness came the bearded figure of Jim Knight.

"Everything all right?" he asked.

"We're all right," said Leon, "but our teacher isn't."

Even though he was hanging in mid-air, Mr Wellington smiled.

"I got stuck," he said.

Jim Knight looked at him as if he was as mad as a box of frogs. Then, without even using the chair, he pulled himself on to the roof and helped Mr Wellington down.

"I can give you some individual climbing lessons if you want to get up on to roofs on a regular basis," Jim Knight told him.

"I was just up there because some girls thought they saw a werewolf," explained Mr Wellington.

"I didn't *think* it!" tutted Jodie. "I saw it actually climbing into the chicken coop!"

Jim Knight dropped down off the roof himself and raised a hand.

"That was me!" he smiled. "I climb into the chicken coop every night to close it and stop the fox that lives in the woods from eating the chickens!"

Mr Wellington let out a long breath.

"There," he said. "That explains it."

But Shea interrupted.

"How about my brother's Spiderman boxer-shorts?" he asked. "They disappeared last year, and everyone's sure a werewolf took them."

"Hold on," said Mr Knight. He disappeared into the boys' chalet. When he came out, he had a cardboard box labelled LOST PROPERTY: BOYS. He reached inside and produced a pair of Spiderman boxer-shorts. The whole class started laughing. Shea wrinkled up his nose at the pants and hung them from the end of his stick. Jim Knight wished everyone a good rest and headed back to the main building. Mr Wellington got out a wet-wipe to clean his hands.

"Time for some sleep," he said.

There were complaining sounds from the children. Saima flapped her hands to get the girls back inside.

"But I'm too frightened to go to sleep now!" announced Jodie.

"Well, you can't still be frightened of the werewolf," Mr Wellington said.

"I'm not," Jodie told him. "I'm frightened of the fox that lives in the woods!"

The Double-Chocolate Cake

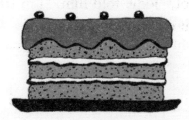

Ivette arrived at school at the same time as Shea. Her bag was on her back and, in her hands, she had something wrapped in tin foil.

"Shea!" she called, as he was about to go through the school gate. "See if Mr Wellington's there!"

Shea looked round.

"Why?" he asked.

"Because it's his birthday and I don't want him to see my mum made this cake."

Shea looked in through the gate and nodded.

"He's there."

"Oh no," sighed Ivette, pressing herself against the wall. "Mum said I've got to keep it a secret, and surprise him when everyone's watching."

"He's going to see it," shrugged Shea.

Ivette shook her head. "I'm going to get it to Sarah in the office," she said. "Then she can keep it until our drama assembly."

"I can tell Mr Wellington to close his eyes for about a minute if you want," suggested Shea.

"No," Ivette tutted.

Shea had another look. "Then it's no use," he told her. "The only way anyone's going to get past without him seeing is in a stealth plane."

Ivette bit her lip and peered cautiously round the wall herself. Then she pulled suddenly back.

"I think he's going!" she said. Shea looked.

"Yep," he said. "He's walking up the steps. He's gone inside."

Ivette waited for a moment. Then she raced across the playground and into the school. She went straight to the school office. But the door was locked. Sarah wasn't there. Even worse, there were footsteps coming. And they were clicky teacher's footsteps. They sounded like Mr Wellington's shoes. Ivette looked in both directions. The nearest doors led into the downstairs hall. She pushed through them and climbed on to the stage. Then she hid the cake, out of sight, in a gap between the back of the stage and the wall. She saw a head through the glass in the door. It *was* Mr Wellington, but he was walking past. Ivette waited. Then she slipped back into the corridor. There were no teachers about, only two boys with their dad. She walked past them and, next thing, was out in the playground again.

She went round making sure everyone in Purple Class knew there was a cake for Mr Wellington hidden at the back of the stage. Some of the children already knew about the cake from Shea. But Ivette told them they all had to keep it a surprise until the end of their drama assembly.

"What sort of cake is it?" asked Yasmin.

"Double-chocolate," Ivette told her.

"That's the best flavour," nodded Zina.

"I wish my mum could learn to make a cake as good as that," said Jodie.

"My mum didn't even just make one,"

Ivette told her. "She made two. One's for my cousin's welcome-home party. When my mum gets baking, you just can't stop her!"

The bell went. The children lined up. Then Mr Wellington appeared and led them into the school. Perhaps because of the secret double-chocolate cake, or perhaps because of the drama assembly, there was a lot of talking going on, and the teacher had to tell the class to quieten down three times.

"Honestly!" he said. "You sound like a hundred monkeys up a tree!"

Leon was chewing a paper-clip and walking just in front of Ivette. As they went down the corridor, he secretively pulled a phone out of his trouser pocket.

"Look," he said, flicking it open.

"Is it yours?" Ivette whispered.

Leon nodded. "There's a film on it with a dog on a skateboard."

He held it up and Ivette saw a sausage dog on a skateboard. It was wearing a baseball cap. They reached the classroom. Leon shut the phone and pushed it into his pocket.

"You've got to leave phones at the office,"

Ivette whispered. "That's the rule."

Leon shifted the paper-clip from one side of his mouth to the other.

"Don't worry," he said. "The ring-tone's on *silent mode*."

***

"Did everyone have a good weekend?" Mr Wellington asked, as the children sat on the carpet. There were some nods.

"It was Jodie's party," said Shea.

Mr Wellington raised his eyebrows and took out the register.

"How was that, Jodie?" he asked.

"It was cool," Jodie told him.

"We played *Dead Man*," added Yasmin.

"That's a cheerful name for a birthday game," nodded Mr Wellington.

"It's Jodie's dad's speciality," went on Jamal. "You turn out the lights. Then he passes bits of a dead man round in a bag and you touch them."

"It sounds revolting," said Mr Wellington.

"It's *good*," Zina told him. "First there was a dried apricot and that was the dead man's ear. Then there were cold sausages and they were his fingers."

"After the fingers it was grapes, and they were his eyes," beamed Shea. "Then it was jelly which was his brains..."

"All right," interrupted Mr Wellington. "I get the picture."

"Then it was warm spaghetti!" called out Jodie, "and that was the worms that were eating him because he's dead!"

"Do we have to talk about this straight after breakfast?" asked Mr Wellington. "I couldn't think of anything worse to play on *my birthday*,"

He paused slightly, as if somebody might remember it was his birthday. But nobody said anything, except for Leon.

"We could play *Dead Man* here sometimes," he suggested.

There was a murmur of agreement.

"It's fun, but also very *educational*," nodded Jodie. "You learn about the different parts of a body dead people have."

"We could get Jodie's dad in as a supply teacher if you're ill, Mr Wellington," pointed out Ivette.

"Or even if you're not ill," added Jamal.

"ALL RIGHT!" said Mr Wellington, glancing at his watch, "Thank you for your suggestions, but we've got a drama assembly to put on in forty-five minutes. The whole school is coming. Miss Zanetos is going to take photographs. And we need to do a run-through."

He took the register. Then the children lined up to go to the downstairs hall. In Literacy they had been writing play-scripts in pairs. Zina and Yasmin had written a play about healthy eating. It was called *Hungry For Success* and that was what the class was going to perform. The main characters were Shea and Yasmin. Shea's character ate five portions of fruit and vegetables every day, but Yasmin's character didn't. Several children were narrators, who explained why healthy eating is important. Other children played different types of fruit and vegetables. Leon was a carrot. Jodie was an onion. Zina was a strawberry.

Mr Wellington watched from the middle of the hall as the children got into position. Zina was the first on to the stage.

"There's the cake!" she whispered, pointing at the gap between the back of the stage and the wall. Straight away, other children wanted to see the cake, and Ivette hissed, "Don't look at it or you'll ruin the surprise!"

They got everything ready for the beginning of the play. The narrators stood at the front. Others, including Shea and Leon, waited out of sight. And, because they were out of sight, Leon took out his phone and showed Shea the skateboarding dog.

"Mr Wellington will get stressed if he finds out you've got that," Shea told him.

"*It's on silent mode*," whispered Leon.

"COME ON!" shouted Mr Wellington, looking at his watch. "Too much dilly-dallying! Too much shilly-shallying! Is everybody ready? Is everybody happy?"

Most of the children nodded, but Jodie didn't.

"I'm ready," she said, "but I'm not happy."

"Well, what's the problem, Jodie?" Mr Wellington asked.

"I don't want to be an onion," Jodie told him.

"Why not," asked Mr Wellington, putting his hands on his hips.

"For personal reasons," Jodie told him.

Mr Wellington scratched his head.

"There's nothing wrong with being an onion," he said. "The onion's the one that does the hoolah-hooping during the song."

"That makes it even *worse*," said Jodie.

Zina put up her hand.

"Jodie wants more of an important part because she's going to be an actress in reality when she grows up," she explained.

"*No*," said Jodie, rolling her eyes, "I'm going to be a singer who also acts and sometimes does perfume adverts."

"Well look, Jodie," said Mr Wellington, "being an onion in our drama assembly isn't going to stop from you doing any of those things later."

"How do *you* know?" Jodie asked him. "In this day and age agents come talent-spotting at school plays. That can be your big break. But if someone comes and sees me as an onion you'll find my future acting career is probably ruined for the rest of my life."

"Oh come on," Mr Wellington told her. "The onion's important. And I tell you what... if Miss Zanetos gets a good photograph of you when you do the hoolah-hooping then that's what I'm going to use as the screensaver on my new laptop."

Jodie blinked as though she wasn't sure whether to be more pleased or disappointed.

"Anyway," Mr Wellington told her. "THERE'S NO TIME LEFT TO DISCUSS WHO'S DOING WHAT! We've got to get practising before the audience arrives!"

He checked that everything was in place, and reminded the children to speak loudly and clearly. Then they started the run-through. It went well. Nobody forgot any lines. The jokes made Mr Wellington smile. It was all looking very good, until the song at the end of the play. In the middle of it, the children had to shout out, "VITAMINS AND MINERALS GIVE YOU ENERGY!"

And, at that moment, Jodie was supposed to start hoolah-hooping energetically, then throw her arms up and smile. But Jodie hoolah-hooped slowly. She didn't throw her arms up. And she looked gloomy.

"JODIE!" called out Mr Wellington. "This is supposed to be the high point of the play and you look as though you've just swallowed an alligator! We're going to do the song again, and this time I want you to give it more OOMPH!"

"How much more OOMPH?" asked Jodie, twiddling with her hoop.

"Ten times more," said Mr Wellington.

The children started the song again. Mr Wellington raised his hands to encourage them to sing louder. They did and, when they got to the middle, they shouted, **"VITAMINS AND MINERALS GIVE YOU ENERGY!"**

At that, Jodie smiled such a big smile it looked as if she had a coat-hanger in her mouth and she began hoolah-hooping faster than before. *Much* faster than before, in fact. And she got quicker, swerving herself this way and that, so the hoop flew round. Then she threw her arms up so energetically that she had to take a step backwards to keep her balance. But she was swerving so much that her foot slipped, the hoop dropped, she stumbled, caught her shoe on the hoop, lost her footing and fell into the gap between the wall and the back of the stage.

Yasmin and Shea reached down to help Jodie get to her feet. Mr Wellington rubbed his face with his hands.

"Jodie! Are you all right?" he asked.

"Yeah," she said, "It's OK. I landed on something soft."

"That was completely over the top!" Mr Wellington told her. "In the performance I don't want that much OOMPH. Do you understand?"

Jodie brushed at her trousers and nodded.

Mr Wellington looked at his watch. Then he shook his head.

"Well that's it," he said. "The audience will be coming any minute, so I need you to *quietly* get everything back into place for the start of the play."

The children began sorting things out. Mr Wellington went to adjust the blinds at the side of the hall and Ivette strode straight to the back of the stage.

"Jodie," she whispered. "If you squashed the cake, my mum's going to kill you and so am I!"

A huddle of children was already gazing down into the gap at the back of the stage.

"That was going to be for Mr Wellington's birthday," blinked Zina.

"I might have dented it," whispered Jodie.

Ivette looked down at the cake. It was squashed sideways. Mushed-up icing and cake was bursting out of the tin foil.

"You've splurged it to bits!" she hissed. Then, as she spoke, Mr Wellington's voice came from the other side of the hall.

"EXCUSE ME! I don't mean to interrupt your discussion group but I said QUIETLY!"

The children carried on setting up the stage.

"Ivette," whispered Jodie. "When's your cousin coming home?"

"Wednesday," Ivette told her.

"Then what about that other cake your mum made?" Jodie went on. "Couldn't your mum bring it in for Mr Wellington and bake a new one for your cousin?"

"My mum's at work," Ivette told her.

"What about your sister?"

Ivette thought for a moment.

"She goes to college at lunchtime," she said. "So... if I could call her now, she'd bring the other cake. It's only round the corner."

"Leon's got a mobile," whispered Shea.

Ivette looked across at Leon. He was straightening a bench at the back of the stage.

"Leon!" she whispered.

"LEON!" called out Shea.

Leon looked round. But so did Mr Wellington.

"RIGHT! THAT'S ENOUGH!" he shouted. "It would be easier to put a t-shirt on an octopus than keep you lot quiet today! And since you can't do this quietly then you're going to do it in silence!"

He walked right up to the edge of the stage and folded his arms. And for one moment, there *was* absolute silence. But then there was a loud BLEEP! BLEEP!

"What was that?" snapped Mr Wellington. "Who's got a phone?"

Leon took the paper-clip out of his mouth and raised his hand.

"Honestly, Leon!" Mr Wellington snapped. "You know the rules."

Leon bit his lip as he took the mobile from his pocket and stared at it.

"It wasn't a phone call – it was a text message,"

he said.

"That doesn't make one bit of difference," said Mr Wellington, holding out his hand. Leon stepped down off the stage and gave the mobile to his teacher.

"This is going straight where it belongs," Mr Wellington announced. He looked at the children up on the stage and said, "Ivette! Take it to the office and come straight back!"

***

It was the first bit of luck Ivette had had all day. She jumped off the stage and Mr Wellington handed her the phone. Then she darted into the corridor and along to the office. Sarah looked up as she walked in. Speaking quickly, Ivette handed over the phone and told Sarah what had happened. The school secretary put it in a drawer. Then Ivette explained why she needed to call her sister.

"Of course you can," Sarah nodded, and passed Ivette the office phone.

Ivette looked happy as she came back into the hall. Red Class was just going in, and there were already five or six other lines of children sitting down. The Purple Class performers were standing next to the stage while Mr Wellington gave them some last reminders.

"Drama is about speaking," he said, "but *listen carefully* as well. Jodie, be sensible with your hoolah-hooping. The rest of you, you've put a lot of effort into this and I'm sure it's going to be very good."

He looked around at the children then added, "Are there any questions?"

Leon put up his hand. "Can you do finger hoolah-hooping with a roll of sellotape?" he asked.

Most of the children managed not to laugh.

"Leon," said Mr Wellington, gesturing for the other children to get up on to the stage, "I admire a questioning mind, but do you think that's an appropriate question?"

"Nope," said Leon getting on to the stage himself. "I just thought you might like to know that I can do it."

***

The drama assembly went down well. Miss Zanetos crouched at the front and took photographs. Shea forgot one of his lines, but Ivette said it for him, so it didn't show. The song was loud and clear. And when Jodie got a round of applause for her hoolah-hooping she looked pleased. At the end, when the clapping had died down, Mr Wellington came to the front of the stage to thank everyone for coming, and Ivette caught sight of Sarah carrying a cake wrapped in tin foil. She tried not to smile as she hurried up the side of the hall to fetch it.

Mr Wellington finished what he had to say, and the audience gave the class another round of applause. Then Ivette came to the front holding the cake. The clapping faded and there was cheering and talking instead. Mr Wellington looked a bit embarrassed, but mainly happy.

"Happy Birthday, Mr Wellington," Ivette told him. "We pretended we didn't know it was your birthday, but we did know. And my mum

made this from everyone in Purple Class because you're our teacher and sometimes your lessons are good."

Everyone clapped again. Mrs Sammy started singing, "HAPPY BIRTHDAY TO YOU..." and the whole school joined in.

When the song was over, Mr Wellington called all his class down from the stage.

"Ivette and the rest of you," he said. "I'm very touched."

Then he started pulling the tin foil from around the cake. The cake was revealed. And Ivette's mouth dropped open. There was a message written in the icing.

"Oh no!" she said. "It was going to be the cake for my cousin's welcome-home party. That message is for her, not for you."

Mr Wellington grinned and said, "Well, it's a lovely message if you ask me."

Then he held the cake out so that everyone could see it and the hall filled with a burst of laughter. On the top of the cake it said,

WE LOVE YOU BABE!

Miss Zanetos took a photograph of Mr Wellington grinning and Ivette, Shea and Jodie standing next to him with their hands over their mouths. And that was the photo Mr Wellington used as the screensaver on his new laptop.

For over fifteen years Sean Taylor has worked as a visiting author and storyteller in schools, encouraging children to write poems and stories. The Purple Class stories spring directly from those visits and all the dramas and funny things he sees going on in classrooms. On a recent visit to a Year Five class he arrived and was told that they had a supply teacher for the day. When the woman on reception checked the supply teacher's name, she started giggling. "He's called Mr Twitchett!" she said. The following month Sean did a follow-up session with the same class and, for a second time, their teacher was away. "Will it be Mr Twitchett again?" he asked. The receptionist checked a piece of paper and started laughing so much she nearly bumped her head on her desk. "No!" she said, "This time it's Mr Shifty!"

Find out more about Sean Taylor at his website –
www.seantaylorstories.com

Purple Class and the Skelington

Sean Taylor

Illustrated by Helen Bate

Cover illustrated by Polly Dunbar

Meet Purple Class – there is Jamal who often
forgets his reading book, Ivette who is the best in
the class at everything, Yasmin who is sick on every school
trip, Jodie who owns a crazy snake called Slinkypants,
Leon who is great at rope-swinging, Shea who knows
all about blood-sucking slugs and Zina who makes
a rather disturbing discovery in the teacher's chair...

Has Mr Wellington died? Purple Class is sure he
must have done when they find a skeleton sitting
in his chair. Is this Mr Wellington's skelington?
What will they say to the school inspector?
Featuring a calamitous cast of classmates,
the adventures of Purple Class will
make you laugh out loud in delight.

Purple Class and the Flying Spider

Sean Taylor

Illustrated by Helen Bate
Cover illustrated by Polly Dunbar

Purple Class are back in four new school stories!
Leon has managed to lose 30 violins, much
to the horror of the violin teacher; Jodie thinks
she has uncovered an unexploded bomb in the
vegetable patch; Shea has allowed Bad Boy,
Purple Class's guinea pig to escape; and
Ivette has discovered a scary flying spider,
just in time for Parent's Evening!

Black and White

Rob Childs

Illustrated by John Williams

Josh is soccer-mad and can't wait to
show off his ball skills to his new classmates.
After all, he is the nephew of Ossie Williams –
the best footballer in the country.

Josh's arrival helps to give shy Matthew
more confidence, but it is not welcomed by
Rajesh, the school goalkeeper and captain.
With important seven-a-side tournaments
coming up, will the players be able to settle
their differences and work together
as a team?

Falcon's Fury
Andrew Fusek Peters and Polly Peters
Illustrated by Naomi Tipping

Hidden treasure ... a secret crime ... the precious eggs
of a bird of prey ... When Jan and Marie discover
who is stealing and selling the eggs of a peregrine
falcon, they suddenly find themselves in danger.
Only the ancient legend of Stokey Castle can
help them – and the falcon will show them the way.

Andrew Fusek Peters' and Polly Peters' exciting
new novel revisits the Klecheks, a family from
the Czech Republic newly settled in Shropshire.
Teenage brother and sister Jan and Marie are
soon unravelling villainy and mysteries,
but they will need even greater courage and
ingenuity to face what is about to happen.

Ghostscape

Joe Layburn

Illustrated by John Williams

When Aisha meets a pale, skinny boy called
Richard in the girls' toilets, she is as surprised
to meet a 1940s boy as he is to see a Somali girl.
Aisha finds herself transported back to the time
of the Blitz, when her school was a sanctuary
for East Enders fleeing the bombing.
But Richard becomes more than just a friendly
ghost; he helps Aisha confront difficulties at home,
where she is torn between two cultures.
When Aisha discovers the horrifying events
of her school's past, she must warn Richard
about what is going to happen – but will
anyone believe her?
Based around true events, Joe Layburn's gritty
story shows how friendship can embrace
differences and change lives.

Night Flight

Michaela Morgan
Illustrated by Erika Pal

A new life should be exciting – but for Danni,
it's a battle. He and his 'aunty' live in a tower block,
with only distant memories of his faraway home.
His new language is proving difficult, he gets bullied,
and he has nightmares. One day, visiting a city farm,
he meets a horse called Moonlight and his heart starts
to heal. But the nightmares are closing in –
until a sad event sparks a magical night that
will transform his life.

Dan and the Mudman
Jonny Zucker

It is Dan's first day in his new school and
already he has had a run-in with Steve Fenton,
the school 'tough guy'. In his last school it didn't
matter that Dan was Jewish – loads of his
classmates were! But here only
Lucy is nice to him.

When Dan makes a mysterious clay figure for
his class presentation, he finds himself zapped back
in time to the 16th century where he encounters
the mystical Golem of Prague. But little does
Dan realise how his life will be thrown into turmoil
as he helps the Golem right wrongs that happened
many years ago – and how, through learning
the lessons of the past, Dan can find a way to
be accepted and to teach all bullies a lesson!